This Little Tiger
book belongs to:

To Jess . . . and to all the ducklings at
Boston Public Garden ~ M A

For Yasmin and Baldrik ~ SE

LITTLE TIGER PRESS
1 The Coda Centre, 189 Munster Road, London SW6 6AW
www.littletiger.co.uk
First published in Great Britain 2014
Text by Mara Alperin • Text copyright © Little Tiger Press 2014
Illustrations copyright © Sue Eastland 2014
Sue Eastland has asserted her right to be identified as
the illustrator of this work under the Copyright,
Designs and Patents Act, 1988
A CIP catalogue record for this book is available from the British Library
ISBN 978-1-84869-037-0
Printed in China
LTP/1400/1311/1015
4 6 8 10 9 7 5 3

The Ugly Duckling

Mara Alperin

Illustrated by Sue Eastland

LITTLE TIGER PRESS
London

It was a sunny spring morning in the farmyard. Mother Duck sat proudly on her nest.

"Come quickly!" she called to the other animals. "My eggs are beginning to hatch!"

Crack! Crack! Crack! Crack!

Out tumbled four perfect little ducklings. They were soft and fluffy and yellow.

Oooh!

Lovely!

"Aren't they just the **sweetest** ducklings ever!" oinked the pig.

"Cheep!
Cheep!"
chirped the baby ducklings.
And Mother Duck gave them
a big cuddle.

But there was one egg left. It was bigger than the others, and strangely speckled. Then it began to crack open. Out popped . . .

two funny feet,

two wobbly wings,

and one bumpy beak.

Mother Duck gasped. He didn't look *at all* like her other baby ducklings!

What a strange little creature!

Such a funny colour!

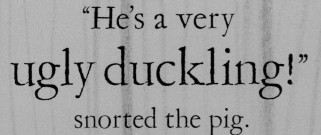

"He's a very **ugly duckling!**" snorted the pig.

"Hush!" scolded Mother Duck. "He's my baby, and I love him.

Now come along, children – it's time for your first swimming lesson."

Mother Duck
marched towards the pond,
and four little ducklings
skipped along behind.

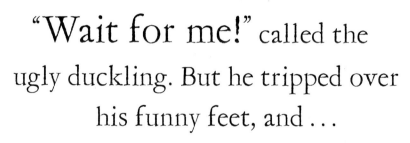

"Wait for me!" called the
ugly duckling. But he tripped over
his funny feet, and . . .

Thump!

Bump!

Thump!

Bump!

. . . he tumbled into the other little ducklings.

How clumsy!

"Never mind," said Mother Duck.
"Now, into the water like good
little ducklings."

"Let's sing our duckling song!" Mother Duck called. "Quackity, quack-quack!"

"Quack! Quack!" chanted the four little ducklings.

"Honkity-honk!" the ugly duckling sang happily.

"What's that?" hooted the horse.
"You don't sing like a duckling!"
"Now, now!" said Mother Duck.
"He'll learn in time."

But the ugly duckling didn't learn. And all
summer long the other animals teased
him when he . . .

got stuck in things . . .

tripped over things . . .

No matter how hard he tried, the ugly duckling
just didn't fit in.

"Why don't you go away!" squawked the other little ducklings. "You're noisy and messy, and you're ruining our fun!"

Just then, they heard Mother Duck calling for her children.

"Not you!" shouted the ducklings.

And off they pranced ... leaving the ugly duckling behind.

"Oh **why** does no one want to play with me?"
sighed the ugly duckling.

"No time to play!" said a mole, popping
his head up. "I'm digging a new
tunnel for the winter."

"Can I help?" asked the
ugly duckling. And he poked
his bumpy beak underground.

"Where are you, my little one?" quacked Mother Duck. "We can't wait any longer – it's time to fly south for the winter."

"I'm coming!" cried the ugly duckling. "Wait for me!"

But the ugly duckling was stuck in the tunnel, and Mother Duck couldn't hear him.

The ugly duckling wriggled and wiggled,
and he pushed and he pulled, until ...

POP!

At last he was free.

But it was too late – they had
left without him.

"Oh no," sniffed the ugly duckling.
"I'll never catch them up now.
I'm all alone."

The days and nights
grew colder, and
the ugly duckling
sheltered in the
hollow of an old
oak tree.

And, as the snowflakes fell,
he curled up in his long wings
and dreamed of sunny days and
games in the meadow.

At last, the sun peeked out,
and the frozen pond
began to thaw.

Then one day, a **beautiful**
swan glided across the
sparkling water.

"Who's there?" called the swan. "Come out and play!"

"I can't," whispered the ugly duckling. "I'm too funny-looking and everybody laughs at me."

The ugly duckling peeked out from behind the reeds. "I wish I could go and swim with her," he said. "But I'm too ugly to be her friend!" And he gave a little sob.

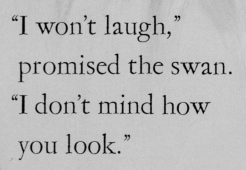

"I won't laugh," promised the swan. "I don't mind how you look."

So the ugly duckling took a deep breath, and stepped outside . . .

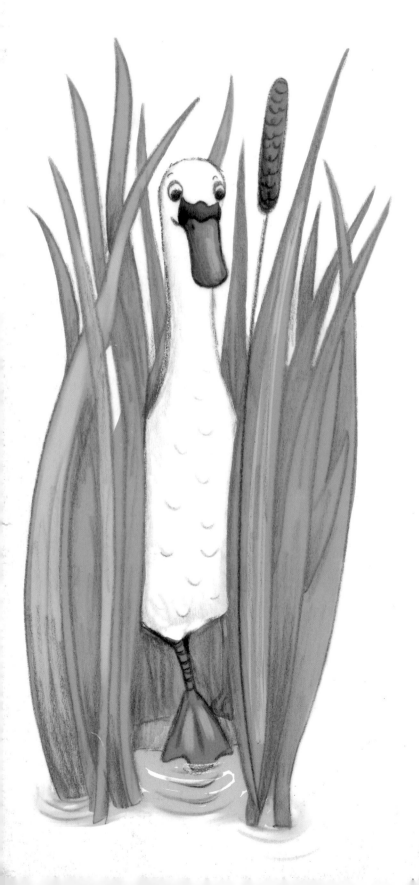

"But you're beautiful!" exclaimed the swan. "Look!"

And he looked down at his reflection . . . and saw that she was right!

The ugly duckling had grown into a swan!
A **beautiful**, **elegant** swan, with dazzling
white feathers and a long,
graceful neck.

So they played together all day. He was very happy indeed – at last he was as beautiful on the outside as he was on the inside.
And best of all, he had
a friend.

My First Fairy Tales

are familiar, fun and friendly stories – with a marvellously modern twist!

The Three Little Pigs — Mara Alperin, Ag Jatkowska

Jack and the Beanstalk — Mara Alperin, Max Chambers

Rumpelstiltskin — Mara Alperin, Loretta Schauer

The Gingerbread Man — Miriam Latimer, Mara Alperin

The Ugly Duckling — Mara Alperin, Sue Eastland

The Elves and the Shoemaker — Mara Alperin, Erica Jane Waters

Chicken Licken — Mara Alperin, Nick East

The Three Billy Goats Gruff — Mara Alperin, Kate Pankhurst

Little Red Riding Hood — Mara Alperin, Loretta Schauer

Goldilocks and the Three Bears — Mara Alperin, Kate Daubney